HARLEY THE HERO

by Peggy Collins

pajamapress

First published in Canada and the United States in 2021

Text and illustration copyright © 2021 Peggy Collins

This edition copyright © 2021 Pajama Press Inc.

This is a first edition.

10 9 8 7 6 5 4 3 2 1

www.pajamapress.ca   info@pajamapress.ca

 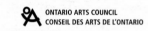

Canada Council   Conseil des arts   ONTARIO ARTS COUNCIL
for the Arts   du Canada   CONSEIL DES ARTS DE L'ONTARIO   Canadä

an Ontario government agency
un organisme du gouvernement de l'Ontario

The publisher gratefully acknowledges the support of the Canada Council for the Arts and the Ontario Arts Council for its publishing program. We acknowledge the financial support of the Government of Canada through the Canada Book Fund (CBF) for our publishing activities.

Library and Archives Canada Cataloguing in Publication
Title: Harley the hero / by Peggy Collins.
Names: Collins, Peggy, 1975- author, illustrator.
Identifiers: Canadiana 20200409875 | ISBN 9781772781953 (hardcover)
Classification: LCC PS8605.O4685 H37 2021 | DDC jC813/.6—dc23

Publisher Cataloging-in-Publication Data (U.S.)
Names: Collins, Peggy, 1975-, author, illustrator.
Title: Harley the Hero / by Peggy Collins.
Description: Toronto, Ontario Canada : Pajama Press, 2021. | Summary: "Harley is a service dog to elementary school teacher Ms. Prichard, who needs a quiet, orderly environment. One of her students, Amelia, has auditory sensitivities of her own. When a small fire throws the class into chaos, Harley must help Ms. Prichard—but he's also the only one who can convince Amelia to come out of hiding"— Provided by publisher.
Identifiers: ISBN 978-1-77278-195-3 (hardcover)
Subjects: LCSH: Service dogs – Juvenile fiction. | Children with disabilities -- Juvenile fiction. | Teachers with disabilities – Juvenile fiction. | BISAC: JUVENILE FICTION / Disabilities & Special Needs. | JUVENILE FICTION / Animals / Dogs. | JUVENILE FICTION / School & Education.
Classification: LCC PZ7.C655Ha |DDC [F] – dc23

Original art created digitally
Letters to Harley created by the students at Selby Public School
Cover and book design—Lorena González Guillén

Printed in China by WKT Company

Pajama Press Inc.
469 Richmond St. E, Toronto, ON M5A 1R1

Distributed in Canada by UTP Distribution
5201 Dufferin Street Toronto, Ontario Canada, M3H 5T8

Distributed in the U.S. by Ingram Publisher Services
1 Ingram Blvd. La Vergne, TN 37086, USA

For SHERRI and STANLEY
And the students and staff
at Selby Public School

And AZALEA and MOWAT
For being amazingly you.

Our class is the quietest, most AMAZING class in the whole school.

That's because Harley is always on the job.

Every day he comes to school in his special blue working vest with Ms. Prichard. His job is to help her feel safe so she can be the best teacher she can be.

He walks beside her, sits beside her, and lies beside her.

He always keeps one eye open
so he can see EVERYTHING.

Harley's a great dog. Most of the time.
Unless he can see your feet.

Harley LOVES to lick feet.
Even though he's on the job,
he just can't resist.

It tickles.
I kind of like it.

Amelia, my very best friend, DOESN'T LIKE it, but she does love Harley. She wears two pairs of socks to school and one pair of rubber boots in the classroom, just in case.

It's MY job to make sure Harley gets to my feet before hers. I'm pretty good at it.

I'm kind of like Harley for Amelia—there are lots of things I do to make her feel safe.

I watch out for things that might upset her like LOUD noises, weird smells, or too-close things. Amelia makes sure my pencils are extra sharp and listens to all my stories.

Other kids don't really get it. HARLEY DOES.

At recess, Harley makes sure everyone is lined up to leave before the teacher says we can go. Amelia and I are always last. It's QUIETER at the end of the line, and there's more SPACE.

At lunchtime I **REALLY** want to pet Harley and feed him my vegetables, but we aren't allowed to do that when he's wearing his vest.

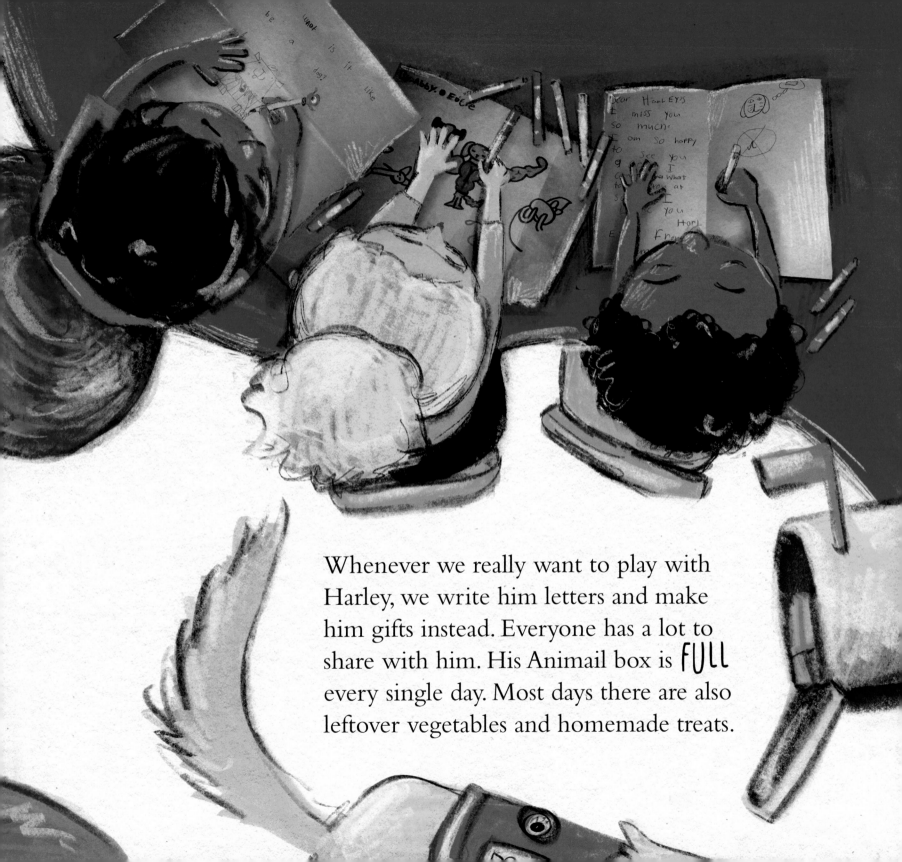

Whenever we really want to play with Harley, we write him letters and make him gifts instead. Everyone has a lot to share with him. His Animail box is FULL every single day. Most days there are also leftover vegetables and homemade treats.

We all love Harley. We also love our teacher, so we make sure everything is QUIET so she can feel safe in our class too.

But **NOTHING** was quiet on the day the old stage curtains caught fire.

Everything was suddenly SO LOUD. The fire alarm rang and rang and rang. It smelled like smoke. There actually WAS smoke.

Everyone ran to the door, even though we were supposed to walk.

Everyone except Amelia.
I saw her run the other way.

"AMELIA!" I yelled.

Ms. Prichard called me to get in line.
"BUT AMELIA IS BACK THERE!" I cried.
My face was wet.

I could hear the fire trucks coming.
HARLEY BARKED AND PULLED HARD
on his leash, dragging Ms. Prichard back to
her desk.

Harley found Amelia under the desk.

He **NUDGED** her.
He **PULLED** on her sleeve.

He **BARKED** in her ear.

Then Harley **LICKED** her boots. Amelia was so startled she jumped out from under the desk.

Ms. Prichard, Amelia, and Harley crawled down the hallway, under the smoke.

Firemen were running around unloading hoses and turning on pumps and already putting the fire out.

When Harley came out with Amelia and
Ms. Prichard, the WHOLE SCHOOL CHEERED!
The firemen cheered too.

Then, as quickly as it
had started, the fire was out.

Everyone was safe.
HARLEY WAS A HERO.

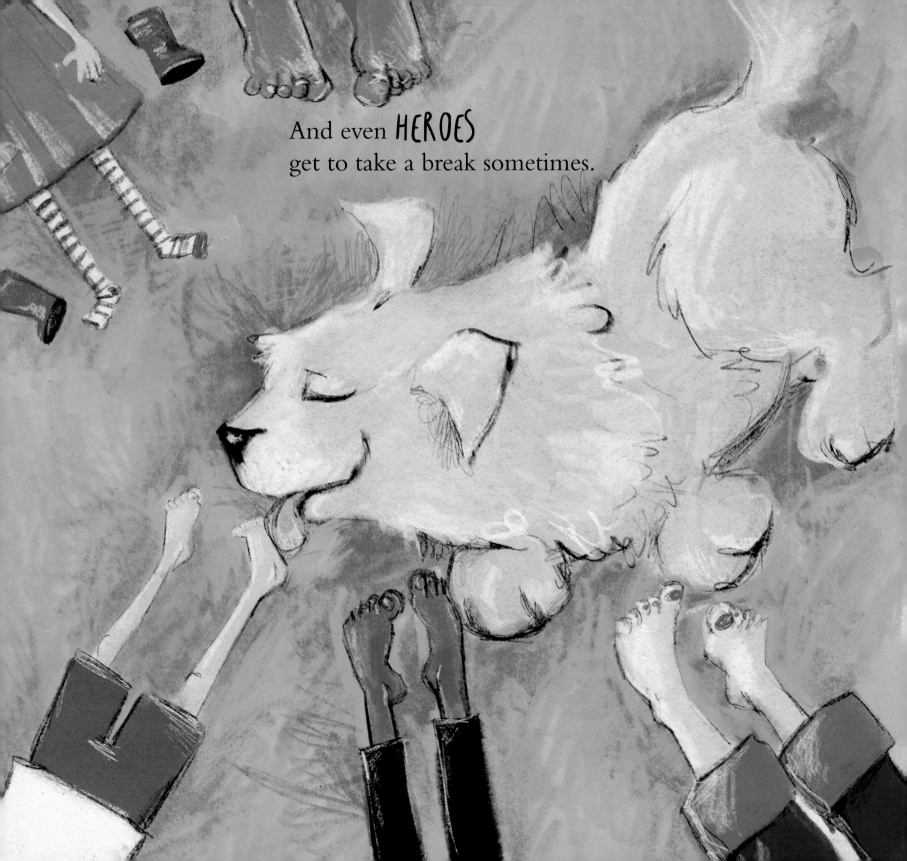

And even HEROES
get to take a break sometimes.

AUTHOR'S NOTE

I visit lots of extraordinary classrooms as an author and illustrator. A few years ago, I visited a classroom at my children's school where the teacher had a service dog named Stanley. I could tell immediately that something about Stanley made this classroom an extra special place. Sherri Richards, the teacher, told me what a difference Stanley made for her and for all the kids. I asked her if I could make a book about Stanley and his adventures, including fire drills, his jobs in the classroom, and the way he really does like to lick toes—even when he isn't supposed to! That story became this book.

A note from Sherri Richards

I am an elementary teacher with Limestone District School Board. I have a service dog named Stanley who was trained by Kingston 4 Paws Service Dogs. He is with me because I have Post-Traumatic Stress Disorder, which is an invisible disability. Students aren't allowed to touch Stanley because he is a service dog, so they interact with him by delivering mail to our classroom "Ani-Mail" box. Kingston 4 Paws helped me train Stanley to open the mailbox, which is a very exciting part of the week in our classroom community. Before I had Stanley, there were years when I couldn't leave my house due to PTSD. He has helped me get my life back and is my true hero!

SHERRI AND STANLEY